Alex and the Magical Flying Coat

By Julia Reid

Illustrated by Amanda Grafe

Leaning Rock Press, LLC

Copyright © 2020 Julia Reid and Amanda Grafe

All rights reserved. No parts of this publication may be reproduced, stored in a database or retrieval system, or transmitted, in any form or by any means,
without the prior permission of the publisher or author, except by a reviewer who may quote brief passages in a review.

Leaning Rock Press, LLC
Box 44
Gales Ferry, CT 06335
www.leaningrockpress.com

978-1-950323-26-5, Hardcover
978-1-950323-27-2, Softcover

Publisher's Cataloging-In-Publication Data
(Prepared by The Donohue Group, Inc.)

Names: Reid, Julia, 1997- author.
Title: Alex and the magical flying coat / by Julia Reid ; illustrated by Amanda Grafe.
Description: Gales Ferry, CT : Leaning Rock Press, [2020] | Interest age level: 004-010. | Summary: Alex has a secret. For generations, his family has possessed a magical flying coat, which they have used to do good in the world. Alex loves to go on adventures with his coat. On his adventure, he encounters a frightening old lady who is lost and begging for help. After denying her, Alex finds himself stuck in a tree and in trouble. His only option is to seek help from the same old lady he denied earlier. Will Alex be saved? What lessons will he learn on this adventure? Find out in this suspenseful book that will leave you wanting to go on your own adventure"-- Provided by publisher.
Identifiers: ISBN 9781950323265 (hardcover) | ISBN 9781950323272 (softcover)
Subjects: LCSH: Coats--Juvenile fiction. | Helping behavior in children--Juvenile fiction. | Magic--Juvenile fiction. | Flight--Juvenile fiction. | CYAC: Coats--Fiction. | Helpfulness--Fiction. | Magic--Fiction. | Flight--Fiction. | LCGFT: Action and adventure fiction.
Classification: LCC PZ7.1.R4547 Al 2020 | DDC [E]--dc23

Printed in the United States of America

To my grandma,
Thank you for the stories, adventures, lessons, cookies, and laughs.
I love you.

Alex's family has a secret.

For generations, Alex's family has possessed a magical coat. It looks just like an ordinary coat, but when someone sits on it with good intentions, it becomes a flying coat.

This year for his birthday, Alex's parents took him aside and said, "Alex, you are an intelligent and mature young man. We are passing this coat on to you, so that you may use it to do good in this world, just as we have done. To make it work, all you have to do is sit on it, with kindness in your heart, and it will take you to someone in need of your help. Use it wisely."

HAPPY BIRTHDAY

One pleasant spring afternoon, after Alex's birthday, Alex was sitting in his room doing his homework when he heard a bird chirping outside his window.

"It is such a beautiful day," he thought. "A quick adventure will help clear my brain. Then I'll be able to finish my work."

Grabbing the magical flying coat, Alex laid it on the floor and sat on it, just as his parents had taught him.

With Alex as its passenger, the coat started to rise up and out of his bedroom window towards the bright sky.

Alex felt the warm breeze on his face and soared high above his neighborhood. Gradually his little town disappeared below him.

As Alex neared the forest, he heard a cry from below. He flew down to get a closer look and saw an old woman crying out for help.

"Please help me!" she said. "I've lost my way."

The woman had a long, pointy nose, warts on her face, and a dirty jacket. Alex was frightened by the way the woman looked, so he pretended he didn't hear her and flew on.

He didn't make it very far, though. Since Alex did not have complete kindness in his heart, the coat began to lose its powers.

As Alex sank towards the forest, his coat got caught on a branch. It was almost as if the tree had reached out to snatch him.

From a branch, Alex yelled loudly, hoping someone would hear him.

"Help!" He screamed.

It was getting close to dinner time, and Alex knew his parents would worry about him if he did not show up on time.

"Help!" He screamed again.

Just then, Alex saw the same woman he had ignored before walking towards him.

"Please help me!" Alex said. "I'm stuck in this tree and need to get home. My parents will wonder where I am".

"Don't worry, young man," the woman called up to him. "I'll help you get down."

Although she looked very old and frail, Alex was surprised when she started to climb the tree. She gently untangled Alex's coat and helped him climb down.

Alex felt guilty for ignoring the woman when she had asked for help. Though he had been frightened by her appearance, she had turned out to be a really nice person.

"I'm sorry for not helping you earlier," Alex mumbled, hanging his head with shame. "Your coat is all dirty and your face has a lot of wrinkles. I was afraid."

The woman lifted Alex's head with her long crooked finger.

"I forgive you," she said. "You are right to be careful of strangers, and if you see someone in need you can always ask an adult what to do. I want you to promise me that you will never judge someone because of the way they look or dress."

"I promise," said Alex.

Together, Alex and his new friend made their way out of the woods.

Recognizing where he was, Alex helped his new friend out of the woods. Then the two friends said their goodbyes and went their separate ways.

Full of kindness and caring, Alex was able to use the magical coat to fly back to his house.

He could not wait to tell his parents about his new friend and the lessons he had learned.

Author

Julia Reid is an author and teacher who lives in Connecticut. She studied Early Childhood Education at Mitchell College, Graduating in 2019. She currently teaches at the Regional Multicultural Magnet School in New London. When she isn't teaching or writing, she enjoys reading, hiking, skiing, yoga, and theater. This is her first children's book, and she hopes to publish many more!

Illustrator

Amanda Grafe is an author and illustrator from New England. She enjoys spending time with her dog, writing about the arts and making the world a better place. She has authored 3 and illustrated 2 children's books: ***My Best Ghoul Friend, Baby Bunny and the Balloon*** and ***The Sneaky Mouse.***

CPSIA information can be obtained
at www.ICGtesting.com
Printed in the USA
LVHW071021050820
661935LV00035BA/1525